Date Due

MAR 1 6 1999		
JUN 2 1 2001		
JUL 2 1 2004		
NOV 05 2005		
DEC 1 5 2014		
FEB 1 8 2016		

BRODART, CO.   Cat. No. 23-233-003   Printed in U.S.A.

The Acorn Tree

and Other Folktales

retold and illustrated by

Anne Rockwell

Greenwillow Books New York

Grateful acknowledgment is made to the following for permission to adapt copyright material:

THE ACORN TREE: From "The Cock and the Hand Mill" in *Russian Fairy Tales* translated by Norbert Guterman, copyright © 1945 by Pantheon Books, Inc., copyright renewed 1973 by Random House, Inc. Adapted by permission of Pantheon Books, a division of Random House, Inc.

THE FLOWER CHILDREN: From "Tale of an Old Woman" in *African Folktales* by Roger D. Abrahams, copyright © 1983 by Roger D. Abrahams. Adapted by permission of Pantheon Books, a division of Random House, Inc.

OWL FEATHERS: From "The Plumage of the Owl" in *The Three Wishes: A Collection of Puerto Rican Folktales* selected and adapted by Ricardo E. Alegría, translated by Elizabeth Culbert (Harcourt, Brace & World, 1969). Adapted by permission of Ricardo E. Alegría.

THE PUPPY-BOY: From "The Puppy Who Became a Boy" in *The Eskimo Storyteller: Folktales from Noatak, Alaska*, copyright © 1975 by The University of Tennessee Press. Adapted by permission of The University of Tennessee Press.

LA-LEE-LU: From "The Singing Geese" in *A Treasury of American Folklore* by B. A. Botkin, copyright © 1944, 1972 by B. A. Botkin. Adapted by permission of Crown Publishers, Inc.

THE TWINS FROM FAR AWAY: From *Pueblo Stories and Storytellers* by Mark Bahti (Treasure Chest Publications, 1988). Courtesy: Treasure Chest Publications.

For
Nicholas,
Julianna,
and Nigel

Serigraphs hand colored with wax-based colored pencils were used for the full-color art.
The text type is Bembo.

Printed in Singapore by Tien Wah Press

First Edition
10 9 8 7 6 5 4 3 2 1

LIBRARY OF CONGRESS CATALOGING-IN-PUBLICATION DATA

Rockwell, Anne F.
The acorn tree and other folktales / retold by Anne Rockwell.
    p.   cm.
Includes bibliographical references.
Contents: The acorn tree—The thirsty crow—The scared little rabbit—The flower children—Owl feathers—The greedy cat—The puppy-boy—The dog and the wolf—La-lee-lu—The twins from far away.
ISBN 0-688-10746-X (trade).   ISBN 0-688-13723-7 (lib. bdg.)
1. Tales.   [1. Folklore.]   I. Title.   PZ8.1.R6Ac   1995
[398.2]—dc20   94-29277   CIP   AC

Author's Note

I don't know how young I was when I first read or heard traditional folktales, but I do know that once I heard one, I was enchanted and wanted more. Folktales invited me into a marvelous world where animals spoke, wishes came true, the impossible could always happen, and what was right won out over what was wrong. I was amazed to discover that these were stories that had been told over and over—ever since people first began to try to understand who they were and how they became that way. They also gave me my first sense of how *ancient* the world was and showed me that the more things changed, the more they remained the same.

This collection is intended to be a beginner's book—a picture book that will introduce a small child to a few of the many classic stories that exist in the world. I have made my choices from traditional stories from many different cultures and have picked those stories I thought would have an immediate appeal for children. While retelling them for young listeners and readers, I have tried to remain true to the meaning of the originals.

Contents

The Acorn Tree

An old man and an old woman lived in a little hut deep in the forest. They were so poor that all they had to eat were the acorns they gathered each day from the forest floor.

One day an acorn fell through a hole in the floor of the little hut. It sprouted green leaves and grew right up through the hole.

"Husband," said the old woman, "we must make this hole bigger so the tree can grow taller."

And so they did. Soon the tree reached the roof.

"Wife," said the old man, "we must cut a hole in our roof so the tree can grow taller."

In no time the tree grew through the roof and up and up until it reached the sky.

The old man and the old woman decided not to gather acorns in the forest that day. Instead they climbed the tree to pick the acorns that grew on its branches, for these were much bigger than the ones they found in the forest.

They climbed and they climbed through the leafy branches of the tree, and after a long, long time they were in the sky. It was very blue.

"How pretty the sky is!" said the old man to the old woman. "Let's walk around and see all we can see."

They hadn't walked very far before they came upon a rooster with a golden comb. He was standing next to a sky-blue grinding mill.

"That sky-blue grinding mill would be very good for grinding acorns," said the old man to his wife. "Then we could use the acorn flour to make good bread."

"The mill doesn't belong to anyone," said the rooster with the golden comb. "Take it, and I will come, too."

So the old man picked up the sky-blue grinding mill and began to climb down the tree. The old woman followed behind him, and so did the rooster with the golden comb.

The three of them climbed down, down, down from the sky. It was almost suppertime when they got to the little hut in the forest.

The old woman put some acorns into the sky-blue grinding mill. Then the old man began to turn the crank. But as soon as he turned it, something remarkable happened. Pancakes and pies popped out of it. They smelled delicious.

"What a wonderful grinding mill!" said the old man and the old woman as they sat down to eat the good pancakes and pies. Of course, the rooster had his share, too. And from that day on they were never hungry.

One day a rich man came riding through the forest. He knocked at the door of the little hut just as the old man, the old woman, and the rooster with the golden comb were sitting down to lunch.

"Won't you have some pancakes and pies with us?" the old woman asked the rich man politely.

The rich man gobbled up a lot of pancakes and pies—first, second, and third helpings.

"What a wonderful thing that grinding mill is!" he said. "I will buy it from you."

"No, it is not for sale," replied the old man and the old woman.

That afternoon, while the old man and old woman were taking their nap, the rich man returned. He sneaked into the house and stole the sky-blue grinding mill. But as he rode off through the forest, the rooster with the golden comb followed him.

As soon as the rich man arrived at his gate, the rooster cried, "Cock-a-doodle-doo! Give us back our sky-blue grinding mill!"

When the rich man heard the rooster say this, he shouted to his cook, "Throw him in the well!"

And the cook did.

But when the rooster with the golden comb landed in the well, he cried, "Little beak, little beak, drink water!"

And he drank up all the water in the well.

Then the rooster flew back to the rich man and cried once more, "Cock-a-doodle-doo! Give us back our sky-blue grinding mill!"

This time the rich man said to the cook, "Roast him on the fire!"

And the cook tossed the rooster with the golden comb onto the fire with all the sausages that were cooking there.

But the rooster cried, "Little beak, little beak, pour water!"

Then all the water from the well poured from his beak and put out the fire.

The cook was very angry to see all the sausages sizzling and smoking before they were done.

The rooster with the golden comb flew right into the dining room, where the rich man and his guests were having dinner. He landed on the rich man's plate, which was piled high with pies and pancakes from the sky-blue grinding mill. "Rich man, rich man, you are a thief!" the rooster cried out.

When the dinner guests heard that, they jumped up from their places at the table and ran straight out of the dining room, for none of them wanted to be friends with a thief.

The rich man ran after them, calling, "Come back! Come back!"

While everyone was out of the room, the rooster picked up the sky-blue grinding mill. He flew right back to the little hut in the forest.

So the old man and his wife and the rooster with the golden comb all had plenty of good pancakes and pies for supper.

As for the rich man, he had no supper at all.

The Thirsty Crow

There was once a very thirsty crow who saw a pitcher of water standing on a table in a garden.

"Caw! Caw!" said the crow. "I will drink that nice, cool water. Then I won't be thirsty anymore."

So the crow flew up to the table. She tried to drink the water from the pitcher. But the water was at the bottom of the pitcher, and no matter how hard she tried, the crow couldn't reach it.

"Caw! Caw! What will I do? I can't reach the water, and I am so very thirsty!" cried the crow.

She looked around the garden and saw some pebbles lying among the flowers.

"Caw! Caw! What a good idea I have!" cried the crow.

She picked up a pebble in her beak and dropped it

into the pitcher. The water at the bottom of the pitcher rose a little.

One, two, three, four, five, six, seven, eight, nine . . . As the crow dropped pebbles into the pitcher, the water rose higher and higher.

When the tenth pebble fell into the pitcher, the water was high enough at last. The thirsty crow stuck her beak in the pitcher and drank the nice, cool water.

"Caw! Caw!" the crow cried as she flew away. "That water was very, very good."

Clever crow!

The Scared Little Rabbit

One morning a little rabbit was nibbling leaves in the jungle, right under a coconut tree.

Thump! Bump!

A big coconut fell out of the tree. It made a very loud noise and a very deep hole in the ground.

The little rabbit was frightened. The earth is caving in, he thought, and he ran away.

He ran past a big rabbit.

"Why are you running so fast?" the big rabbit asked.

"The earth is caving in!" cried the little rabbit. "Run! Run!"

The big rabbit was frightened, too, and he began to run.

The little rabbit and the big rabbit ran and ran. They ran past a jackal.

"Why are you running so fast?" the jackal asked.

"The earth is caving in!" cried the little rabbit and the big rabbit. "Run! Run!"

Now the jackal was frightened, and she began to run, too.

The little rabbit and the big rabbit and the jackal ran and ran. They ran past two monkeys.

"Why are you running so fast?" the monkeys asked.

"The earth is caving in!" cried the little rabbit and the big rabbit and the jackal.

"Then we'd all better run!" said the two monkeys, and they did.

The little rabbit, the big rabbit, the jackal, and the two monkeys ran and ran. They ran past a tiger cub.

"Why are you running so fast?" the tiger cub asked.

"The earth is caving in!" cried the little rabbit, the big rabbit, the jackal, and the two monkeys.

A huge elephant overheard them. "I think we should go and tell the king," the elephant said.

So the tiger cub and the huge elephant joined the little rabbit, the big rabbit, the jackal, and the two monkeys, and they all ran as fast as they could, looking for the king.

Soon they came to a lion who was walking through the jungle very peacefully. The lion was the king of the jungle.

"Oh, King," cried the little rabbit, the big rabbit, the jackal, the two monkeys, the tiger cub, and the huge elephant when they saw the lion. "We were looking for you. We want to tell you that the earth is caving in."

"How do you know this?" asked the lion.

"The little rabbit told us so," said the big rabbit, the jackal, the two monkeys, the tiger cub, and the huge elephant.

"Show me," said the lion.

They all ran back through the jungle. They ran until they came to the place where the little rabbit had been nibbling leaves under the coconut tree. It was very quiet there.

The lion looked around and saw a big coconut lying in a hole in the ground. "Did you hear a loud thump?" he asked the little rabbit.

The little rabbit nodded.

"And an even louder bump?" said the lion.

Again the little rabbit nodded.

"Little rabbit," the lion said kindly, "the noise you heard was not the earth caving in. It was just the sound this big coconut made when it fell from the tree and hit the ground. There's no need to be frightened."

And when they heard this, the little rabbit, the big rabbit, the jackal, the two monkeys, the tiger cub, and the huge elephant went back to whatever they had been doing that morning.

And the lion continued walking peacefully through the forest.

The Flower Children

Once there was a woman who had no family. She had no husband, no mother or father. She had no brothers or sisters, no nieces or nephews, and she had no children to call her Mother. She lived all by herself.

Every day she took her ax and went into the forest to chop wood, which she sold to people in the village. But because she had no family, none of the villagers treated her with respect.

One day, when the woman went deeper into the forest than usual, she found a tree whose branches were covered with beautiful flowers. It was unlike any tree she had ever seen. The woman didn't know it, but that tree was a magic tree. She picked up her ax and began to chop it down.

Suddenly the tree cried out, "Stop! Stop! Why are you cutting me with your sharp ax? What have I ever done to hurt you?"

"Just what have you ever done for me? Can you tell me that?" the woman replied.

She didn't even wait for an answer. Instead she chopped, chopped, chopped even harder.

The magic tree said, "Oh, please, please don't hurt me anymore. If only you will stop chopping, I promise I will do something good for you."

The woman said, "What can you do for me? You are only a tree."

The tree said, "Look up into my branches."

The woman looked up, then said, "All I see are flowers."

"If you will stop hurting me with your sharp ax," said the tree, "all those flowers can be your children. They will call you Mother."

The woman who had no family thought it would be wonderful to have so many children. So she put her sharp ax on the ground and promised the tree that she would chop no more.

No sooner had she spoken than all the flowers turned into children—boys and girls, big and little. They came climbing down through the branches, crying, "Mother! Mother, take us home!"

The woman was very happy. "Come along, children. Follow me. It is almost time for lunch," she said.

She let the biggest child carry her sharp ax. "You be careful now," she said. "Don't hurt yourself."

"No, Mother, I won't," said the biggest child.

Then the woman took the hands of the two littlest children, and they started on their way home.

"Wait," called the magic tree. "You must make me one promise."

"What is that?" asked the woman.

"You must promise that you will never be cross with any of the children and that you will never, ever scold a single one of them."

The woman looked at all the beautiful children who now called her Mother. She smiled and said, "Of course, I will never be cross and scold them. Why would I do such a thing?"

"Very well," said the tree. "But don't forget your promise."

The next morning, when the woman went to market to sell wood, all her children went with her. Everyone in the village stared as she walked by. They said, "What beautiful children that woman has!" And from that day on they looked at the woman with new respect.

The children were good as well as beautiful. They helped the woman plant a garden, and she sold what they grew at the market. She didn't have to go to the forest to chop wood anymore. The children laughed and played all day long and made the woman happy.

But one day the littlest child said, "Mother, I am hungry. Feed me."

The woman was cooking a good soup on the fire, but it was not done. So she said, "Your soup is not ready yet. Go play with your brothers and sisters, and I will call you when the food is cooked."

But the littlest child began to cry and tug at the woman's skirt, saying, "I want it now! I want it now!"

And then all the other children began to say, "We want some soup, too, and we want it now! We are hungry! Feed us!"

They made a lot of noise with their crying and clamoring. How that woman wished they would be quiet! She forgot all about the promise she had made to the magic tree. She scolded the children in a cross voice, saying, "Don't you bother me! Be quiet, all of you, and wait until I'm ready to feed you!"

Of course, she was not saying anything she had not heard the villagers say to their children. But no sooner had she said it than all the children turned back into flowers.

Each flower drifted away in the breeze. They drifted all the way through the forest until they reached the magic tree, where they settled on the branches. And they are blooming there still.

Day after day the woman who forgot her promise went to the forest. She searched everywhere for the magic tree covered with the flowers that had been her beautiful children. But she never found it. And to this day neither has anyone else.

Owl Feathers

A long time ago animals used to give parties and balls, just as people do. One day the birds decided to have a ball. Birds from everywhere in the world were invited to come, wearing their finest feathers. Hawk was in charge of delivering the invitations, for in those days he was the most polite bird in the world.

Hawk set off around the world and delivered each invitation personally. He invited the dove and the flamingo, the rooster and the sparrow, the duck and the parrot. He invited big birds and small birds, chattering birds and birds with beautiful songs, birds with bright feathers and birds that were gray and brown.

When Hawk came to Owl's house, he gave him the invitation to the ball, as he had the other birds.

Owl read it and then said sadly, "I cannot come."

"Why not?" asked Hawk.

"Well, just look at me," said Owl. "Don't you see that I have nothing to wear?"

Hawk looked at him and noticed that Owl was completely naked. He had no feathers at all on his body, not a single one. He was quite dismal-looking, in fact.

Hawk felt sorry for Owl and said, "Don't worry. I will talk with my friends, and we'll see what we can do to get you something to wear to the ball."

Hawk told the other birds that Owl couldn't come to the ball because he had nothing to wear. "I will lend him one of my feathers," said Dove, who was very kind.

"I will lend him one of mine," said Duck.

"And I will lend him one of my shiny ones," said Rooster.

Soon all the birds had promised to lend Owl feathers to wear to the ball. On the day of the ball Hawk carried the feathers to Owl's house.

When Owl saw all the many beautiful feathers Hawk had brought him, he said, "How can I ever thank you, my friend?"

"Don't thank me," said Hawk. "Thank my friends the other birds instead."

But Owl paid no attention to him. He was too busy dressing up in the feathers and admiring his reflection in the lake.

Hawk said good-bye to Owl. "See you at the ball," Hawk said. "And by the way, don't forget, my friends are only lending you their feathers. They're not giving them to you to keep. You have to give each feather back to its owner as soon as the ball is over. Don't forget."

Owl promised Hawk he would do that. But when the night of

the ball arrived, he could hardly enjoy the dancing. All he could think about was that he had to return the beautiful feathers he was wearing. And he didn't want to.

None of the dancers noticed when Owl left the ball. He hid in the forest, in a dark hole in a tree where none of the other birds could find him.

The next morning the birds went looking for Owl. They called, "Owl, where are you? Give us back the feathers you borrowed from us."

But no matter how loudly they called, Owl didn't answer. At last all the birds had to go back to wherever they belonged without the fine feathers they had loaned to Owl, and each one of them was very angry at him for breaking his promise.

From that time to this, birds still spend part of every day looking for Owl. That's why Owl never comes out in the daytime. He stays hidden in his dark hole in the tree until it is night, when the other birds are asleep.

And late at night he comes out and dances all alone. He looks very handsome in his fine feathers, but only the moon and stars can see him.

As for Hawk, he has never again done a kind thing for anyone.

The Greedy Cat

Once upon a time there was a very greedy cat. No matter how much his master fed him, the cat always wanted more. So one day the master decided to send the cat away before he ate him out of house and home.

He gave the cat a bowl of porridge and a platter of bacon, then shooed him out and locked the windows and door.

The cat had gobbled down the bowl of porridge and the platter of bacon, but he was still hungry and started off in search of more to eat.

Soon he met a hen.

"Good day to you, Cat," said the hen. "And how is life treating you these days?"

"Oh, I'm nearly starving to death," said the cat. "All I've eaten today is a bowl of porridge and a platter of bacon, so I think I'll eat you, too."

And the greedy cat swallowed the hen, just like that.

He continued on his way until he met a milkmaid.

"Good day to you, Cat," said the milkmaid. "And how is life treating you these days?"

"Oh, I'm nearly starving to death," said the cat. "All I've eaten today is a bowl of porridge, a platter of bacon, and a hen, so I think I'll eat you, too."

And the greedy cat swallowed the milkmaid, just like that.

Across the meadow was a cow.

"Moo! Good day to you, Cat," called the cow. "And how is life treating you these days?"

"Oh, I'm nearly starving to death," said the cat. "All I've eaten today is a bowl of porridge, a platter of bacon, a hen, and a milkmaid. So I think I'll eat you, too."

And the greedy cat swallowed the cow, just like that.

By this time the cat was getting very, very fat. But he walked along until he met a sly fox.

"Good day to you, Cat," said the sly fox. "And how is life treating you these days?"

"Oh, I'm nearly starving to death," said the cat. "All I've had to eat today is a bowl of porridge, a platter of bacon, a hen, a milkmaid, and a cow. So I think I'll eat you, too."

"Oh, I wouldn't do that if I were you," said the sly fox. "Why don't you eat the wolf? He is much bigger and tastier than I am, and he is just around the bend in the road through the forest."

Since the cat was feeling mighty hungry and the fox was rather small, he said, "Thank you for your good advice, my friend."

Then the fat, greedy cat went down the road and around the bend into the forest.

Soon he met a wolf.

"Good day to you, Cat," said the wolf. "And how is life treating you these days?"

"Oh, I'm nearly starving to death," said the cat. "All I've had today is a bowl of porridge, a platter of bacon, a hen, a milkmaid, and a cow. So I think I'll eat you, too."

And the greedy cat swallowed the wolf, just like that. But he still wasn't satisfied and went on through the forest.

Before long he met a woodchopper who carried an ax.

"Good day to you, Cat," said the woodchopper. "And how is life treating you these days?"

"Oh, I'm nearly starving to death," said the cat. "All I've eaten today is a bowl of porridge, a platter of bacon, a hen, a milkmaid, a cow, and a wolf. So I think I'll eat you, too."

And the greedy cat swallowed the woodchopper, ax and all, just like that.

Soon he met a brown bear.

"Good day to you, Cat," said the brown bear. "And how is life treating you these days?"

"Oh, I'm nearly starving to death," said the cat. "All I've had to eat today is a bowl of porridge, a platter of bacon, a hen, a milkmaid, a cow, a wolf, and a woodchopper and his ax. So I think I'll eat you, too."

And the greedy cat swallowed the brown bear, just like that.

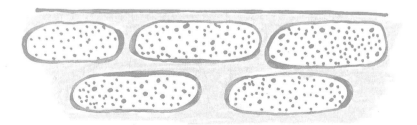

By now the cat was so fat he could hardly walk. But he was still looking for more to eat.

Finally he came to a bridge over a river. A big, rough, tough billy goat with two strong horns was standing on the bridge.

"Good day to you, Cat," said the billy goat. "And how is life treating you these days?"

"Oh, I'm nearly starving to death," said the cat. "All I've had to eat today is a bowl of porridge, a platter of bacon, a hen, a milkmaid, a cow, a wolf, a woodchopper and his ax, and a brown bear."

The fat and greedy cat looked at the big billy goat standing on the bridge. He looked very tasty indeed. So the cat said, "I'm so hungry I think I'll eat you, too."

But the big, rough, tough billy goat said, "Just you try it! If you come walking onto my bridge, I'll butt you once and I'll butt you twice with my big strong horns until I butt you right into the river."

Well, the cat paid no attention. He walked onto the bridge to gobble up that big billy goat.

The big, rough, tough billy goat did exactly what he had said. He butted that big, fat, greedy cat with his big, strong horns. The cat went up in the air, over the bridge, and into the river. He landed with a splash and a crash.

And when that big, fat, greedy cat landed with a splash and a crash, he hiccuped. Out came the hen, the milkmaid, the cow, the wolf, the woodchopper and his ax, and the brown bear, too.

All of them ran off as fast as they could go.

The greedy cat was left with nothing in his stomach but the bowl of porridge and the platter of bacon. So off he went to search for something more to eat.

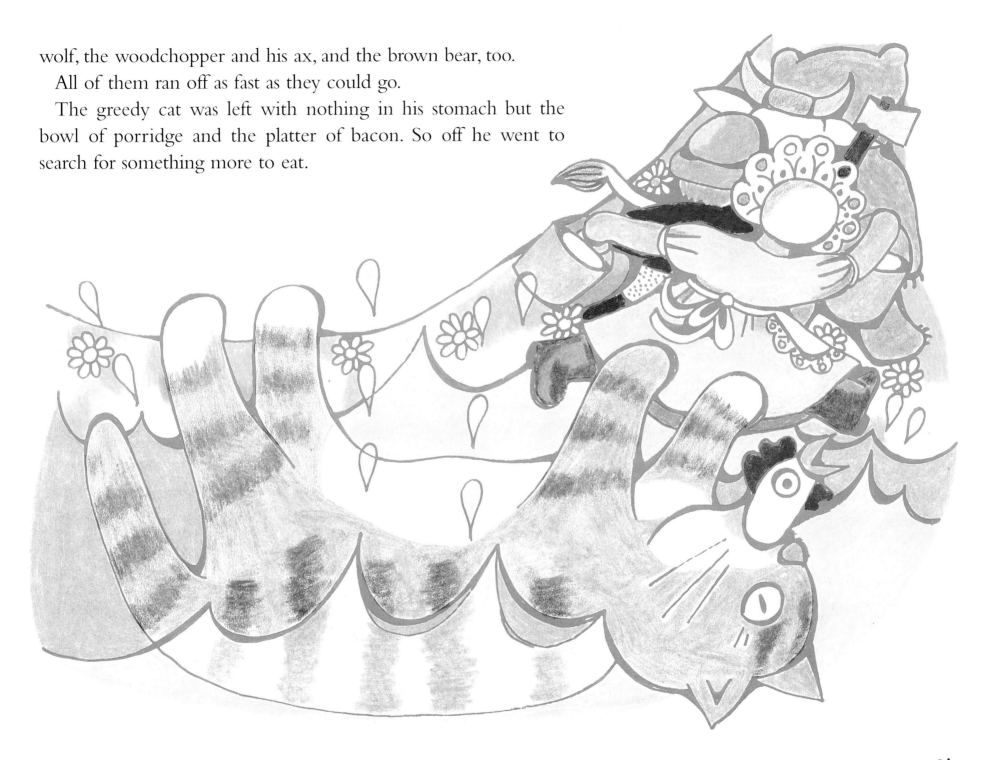

The Puppy-Boy

A man and his wife lived way up north. The man had never been a lucky hunter, not even when he was young. Now that he was old, he caught next to nothing. And because he and his wife had never had any children, there was no strong young person to help him.

One day the man felt so discouraged he decided not to go hunting in the icy sea. Instead he just walked along the beach, singing sad songs to himself.

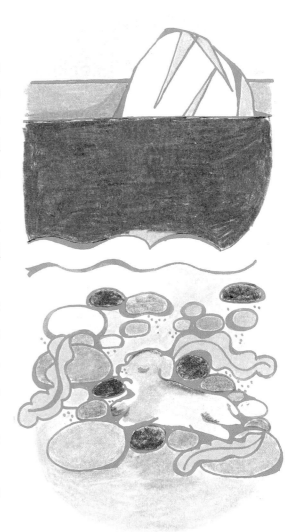

After he had walked many miles, he saw a little newborn puppy lying stiff and cold on the gray beach pebbles. The hunter felt very sorry for the little puppy, so he picked him up, tucked him into his warm parka, and carried him home.

"Look at this poor little puppy I found on the beach," the man said to his wife.

"He looks almost frozen to death," she said. "Let's put him by the fire so he can get warm."

For a long time the puppy lay by the fire without

moving. But toward evening he stretched and made the little whimpering sounds that puppies make. The man and his wife fed the puppy, and before long he started walking around. They stayed up all night with him, and by morning the puppy was playing with the hunter's leather ball, biting it and growling the way puppies do.

"What a pretty puppy we have!" said the hunter to his wife.

"And he is very strong and healthy now," she said.

Every day the puppy grew bigger. But one day he was nowhere to be found. Instead the hunter and his wife saw a little baby boy lying by the door. They were happy and excited, and the woman ran to the baby.

But as soon as she hugged him, he jumped out of her arms and said, "Woof! Woof!" to her. The baby had turned back into their puppy.

The puppy grew bigger until one day he once again couldn't be found. This time the hunter and his wife saw a little boy standing by the door. They ran toward him, but just as the man touched the boy's hand, he barked and became a puppy again.

After a long time had passed, once more the hunter and his wife could not find their puppy. This time a bigger boy was standing at the door. When they ran to him and took his hand, the boy said, "Mother, make me a warm sealskin parka and a pair of boots and some fur mittens, for I want to go outside and play."

And so the woman did.

The next morning the boy said to the hunter, "Father, make me a

toy whaleboat and a toy spear, for I want to go outside and play."

And so the man did.

Then the boy who had been a puppy went out in his new parka, his boots, and his mittens and played at fishing with his toy whaleboat and spear. But soon he caught a real whale. And that whale was enough food for the boy and his mother and father all winter long.

The man and his wife were very glad they had warmed and fed the little frozen puppy the man had found lying on the beach. At last they had a son.

The boy was always a lucky hunter when he played outside in his toy whaleboat with his toy spear. And when he grew up, he remained a lucky hunter and took good care of his father and mother for the rest of their lives.

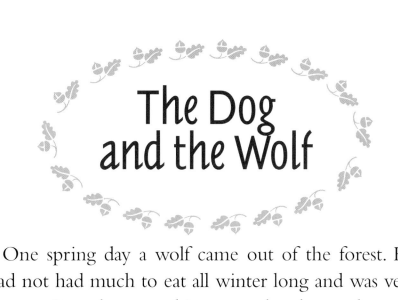

The Dog and the Wolf

One spring day a wolf came out of the forest. He had not had much to eat all winter long and was very hungry. Soon he met a big, strong, handsome dog.

"Good morning, sir," said the wolf to the dog. "You look very happy and well fed. Where have you found food this cold winter?"

"Ah!" said the dog. "I am very fortunate. I do not have to find food. My master feeds me."

The wolf looked suspiciously at the dog. "Hmm," he said. "What do you have to do for this master who feeds you so well?"

"Not much," answered the dog. "I must go for walks with him, and fetch sticks and bring them to him, and sleep in front of the fire by his chair, and be faithful to him, always. I tell you, my friend, it's not at all a bad life. Last night I had roast beef, boiled potatoes, breast of chicken, and a piece of cheese for supper." The dog licked his chops, remembering his good dinner. "Oh, yes," he added, "and I have my own dish to eat from."

"Don't tell me about such delicious things!" cried the wolf. "It makes my stomach growl just to hear you. How fortunate you are!"

"Come with me," said the dog. "You look a little like a dog, and after a good meal and a bath and brushing I am quite sure my master would give you to his servant."

"Oh, how can I thank you?" said the wolf as he loped along beside the dog toward the master's house.

Then the wolf noticed something around the dog's neck that shone in the sun. "What is that you are wearing around your neck?" he asked.

"Oh, that," replied the dog. "That is nothing; it is only my collar."

"And what is a collar? Why do you wear it?" asked the wolf.

"No reason," said the dog. "It is only something my master uses when he chains me up in the yard at night."

"Chains you up!" shouted the wolf. "Do you mean to tell me that you are tied up at night? I love to roam through the forest by moonlight. If I come home with you, would I have to be chained up like you?"

"Of course," answered the dog. "Believe me, that is a small price to pay for all the good things my master gives me. Hurry up, my friend. It is almost time for lunch."

But the wolf did not hear him, for he had run away.

"Chained up all night," muttered the wolf to himself as he ran back to the forest. "I would rather go hungry and have my freedom than be well fed and chained up like that!"

La-Lee-Lu

One day a man went out with his gun to hunt for something for dinner. He saw a great flock of geese flying above him.

They all were singing, "La-lee-lu, come quilla, come quilla, bung, bung, bung, quilla bung," just as loud as can be.

The man aimed up at the flock. Bang! Down fell a nice, plump goose.

But as the goose fell from the sky, she sang, "La-lee-lu, come quilla, come quilla, bung, bung, bung, quilla bung."

The man was mighty surprised to hear that goose still singing as she fell. All the same, he picked her up, put her in his sack, and carried her home for dinner.

When his wife began to pluck the goose, she was astonished to see each feather fly out the window all by itself. And when she put the goose in the oven, the

wife was even more surprised to hear the goose continue to sing, "La-lee-lu, come quilla, come quilla, bung, bung, bung, quilla bung," as it cooked.

When the goose was done, the woman put the bird on the platter and set the platter on the table. Then she and her husband sat down to dinner.

But as soon as the man picked up his carving knife and fork, the goose began again to sing, "La-lee-lu, come quilla, come quilla, bung, bung, bung, quilla bung."

And right at that moment there was a tremendous noise, and a whole flock of geese flew in through the window.

All the geese were singing, loud as can be, "La-lee-lu, come quilla, come quilla, bung, bung, bung, quilla bung."

Each goose was carrying a feather in its beak, and each one stuck its feather in the goose that was lying on the platter, ready for dinner.

Then that goose flew up from the table and right out the window with the others, and they all flew off singing, "La-lee-lu, come quilla, come quilla, bung, bung, bung, quilla bung."

The Twins from Far Away

Long ago there lived a man and his wife. Every morning they gave thanks to the sun for shining on them and prayed for a child of their own.

One morning they heard a baby cry. Four times it cried, but they couldn't tell where the sound came from.

"You go this way and look," said the woman.

"Yes, and you go that way and look," said the man.

So he went north and she went south to look for the baby they had heard crying.

Before long the man and the woman came back to their village, each carrying a strong, healthy baby boy. Each baby boy looked exactly like the other. They were twins, even though one came from the north and one from the south.

The man and his wife thought surely someone would come looking for the babies, so they went to the village leader for advice. He said, "Wait four days. Then, if no one comes to claim them, the babies will be yours."

Four days passed, and no one came to claim the baby boys. The woman and her husband were very happy, for now the children were theirs.

The twins who came from far away grew fast. Soon they had learned all that their mother and father could teach them. But they were different from the village children. They never played with the others, only with each other.

"Those twins are very strange," a woman in the village said. "My mother told me that they eat flowers and dance with butterflies."

"So I have heard," said an old man. "I have also heard that they know how to speak with wild animals."

"They never want to play with me," a little girl said. "And they always tell each other their dreams but never share them with me or my friends."

What she said was true. The twins did have remarkable dreams. From their dreams they learned many things that no one else knew.

Their mother and father understood that their sons were special children, and one day they let them go alone on a journey.

After four days the twins returned. But they had changed. They were grown men now. They had painted their bodies black and white, and they wore yellow and green corn husks in their hair. They laughed and teased and clowned around, and before long all the people in that village were laughing at them.

"What wonderful, funny clowns those twins are!" everybody said, and laughed some more.

Except one person.

There was a man in the village who was a witch-man. All the villagers, even the leader, were afraid of him, for he knew a great deal of evil magic. He had often caused terrible things to happen when he was angry.

This witch-man hated to hear his neighbors happily laughing at the twins. He tried many ways to make something bad happen to the brothers, but he couldn't. That was because they, too, knew magic, but theirs was good magic, and it protected them.

One day the witch-man said to the twins, "Let's have a contest to see who can make the best magic. Whoever loses will have to leave this village forever."

Both brothers immediately accepted his challenge.

On the day of the contest all the people gathered in the plaza to watch.

The witch-man brought a large pottery jar and placed it upside down in the center of the plaza. He commanded water to flow from the jar, and flow it did. It flowed like a wide river all around, all through the plaza. Then it disappeared. Where water had been, corn, beans, and squash sprouted, flowered, and ripened.

But even as the people watched this wonderful magic, all the plants the witch-man had brought forth withered and died. Soon the plaza looked just as it always had.

The twin from the north said to him, "I must admit, that was powerful magic."

The witch-man was flattered. He could hardly keep from smiling smugly.

"Yes," said the twin from the south. "My brother is right. It was wonderful magic. But isn't it too bad you couldn't make it last?"

When the people heard this, they began to make fun of the witch-man because he couldn't make his magic last, and this made him very, very angry.

"Now it is your turn!" he screamed at the twins. "Do you really believe you can do better?"

The twins said, "We will try."

Then the twin from the south said to his brother, "Little brother, bring me some ashes, so that I can make a rain cloud."

And the twin from the north did. Then the twin from the south took the ashes and blew on them. He blew so hard that his brother began to sneeze and cough. All the people laughed, but no rain cloud came.

Then the twin from the north took all the ashes that were left and threw them up into the air. The ashes fell down on both the twins and made their shiny black hair all gray. The people laughed again, for the twins looked funny. Still, not a single cloud appeared in the sky.

Finally the brothers sat down quietly together in the plaza and began to talk, and this was part of their magic, too. Their voices grew softer and softer. Soon all the people became very quiet, so they could hear what the twins were saying.

The twins talked about the many different clouds they had seen. Then they talked about the color of rainbows, about the roar of thunder and the bright flash of lightning. They talked about how sweet the earth smelled when it was wet, and how lovely and green the growing things were that always sprouted after the good rain came. And the words they spoke were as beautiful as the things they spoke of.

Pretty soon one twin stopped speaking. He cupped his hands and puffed out his cheeks, then blew into his hands. A great cloud rose from them. Everyone watched the cloud grow larger and blacker until it covered all the blue sky above the plaza. Rain began to come down hard. Soon thunder roared while bright lightning danced through the dark cloud. All the people ran into their houses.

Except the witch-man. He was so frightened of the magic thunder and lightning the twins had made that he ran away and never came back to the village.

Next morning the wet earth smelled good. All around the village the ground was covered with green growing things—squash and beans and corn. And this magic did not disappear the way the witch-man's had. No, instead the growing things flowered and grew ripe, and the people were able to harvest them.

After the contest the twins who came from far away were chosen leaders of the village, and they ruled wisely together for many years.

1. THE ACORN TREE is a type of story common in European folklore that features miraculous help or wish fulfillment through a magical object or animal. I have adapted it from one of the Russian stories collected by Aleksandr Afanas'ev, "The Cock and the Hand Mill," as translated by Norbert Guterman in *Russian Fairy Tales.*

2. THE THIRSTY CROW is my retelling of a fable from Aesop. When I first heard this tale as a small child, it made an extraordinary impression on me, for it assured me that if you just thought hard enough and didn't give up, you, like the clever crow, could solve almost any problem.

3. THE SCARED LITTLE RABBIT is one of the Jataka tales, that vast collection of animal fables told in India that illustrate the teachings of the Buddha (who in this story is represented by the good lion). But other versions of the story can be found in folklore from as far away as China and Tibet and as near as the tales of Joel Chandler Harris in the United States.

4. THE FLOWER CHILDREN is adapted from "Tale of an Old Woman" in *African Folktales: Traditional Stories of the Black World* selected and retold by Roger D. Abrahams. This tale is attributed to the Bondei tribe, but African folklore contains many stories of trees whose flowers are really children.

5. OWL FEATHERS is a tale from Puerto Rico, but stories of why the owl only comes out at night can be found throughout Latin America and the Caribbean. In all of them, the owl seems to be a somewhat unreliable bird. My story is adapted from "The Plumage of the Owl" in *The Three Wishes: A Collection of Puerto Rican Folktales* selected and adapted by Ricardo E. Alegría.

6. For centuries people have laughed at cumulative tales like THE GREEDY CAT. I based my retelling on "The Tabby Who Was Such a Glutton," one of the traditional Scandinavian stories collected in the nineteenth century by Asbjornsen and Moe. Translations of the story can be found in numerous anthologies.

7. I have always been fascinated by the harsh life and beautiful crafts of the Inuit, those people of the far north who are sometimes called Eskimos. THE PUPPY-BOY is adapted from "The Puppy Who Became a Boy" in *The Eskimo Storyteller: Folktales from Noatak, Alaska* by Edwin S. Hall, Jr.

8. The seventeenth-century French poet Jean de la Fontaine wrote satirical fables in verse about the perils and prizes of life in the luxurious court of Louis XIV, the Sun King. THE DOG AND THE WOLF is my own prose translation of one of La Fontaine's fables.

9. LA-LEE-LU comes from the oral tradition of the southern United States. I adapted it from a story entitled "The Singing Geese" in *A Treasury of American Folklore* edited by B. A. Botkin. The tale had been collected early in this century by Annie Weston Whitney and Caroline Canfield Bullock and first published in *Folk-Lore from Maryland* (Memoirs of the American Folk-Lore Society, Volume XVIII, 1925).

10. THE TWINS FROM FAR AWAY is a Native American tale from the people of the Cochiti Pueblo in what is now New Mexico. Among the pueblos, there are many stories of wise clowns and of miraculous twins who come from different points on the compass. I like this one because it convinces me that beauty—in this case the beauty of life-giving rain—can be created by simply imagining it. My story is adapted from one in *Pueblo Stories and Storytellers* by Mark Bahti.